One Night Love

Whiskey Run Sugar

Hope Ford

One Night Love © 2022 by Hope Ford

Editor: Kasi Alexander

Cover Design: Cormar Covers

Cover Models: Laurel Shada & Jake Beaudin

Image Photographer: Lindee Robinson Photography

Chapter 1

April

"Carrie?" the man asks.

I shake my head, already over this game he's playing.

"Katherine?"

Again, I smile but shake my head. It's a small smile. I don't want to encourage him, but I also don't want to hurt his feelings. I'd been at the bar, sitting at a table close to the entrance for less than five minutes when the man introduced himself as Thomas and sat down next to me. He's nice enough and friendly in a funny way. But I'm not interested. I know I shouldn't judge a man by what he looks like. Heck, I hate it when a man looks at my curves and I see the judgment on his face. Which is why I'm being nice. But the truth is, I like a man that is big. Bigger than me with broad shoulders, a wide chest, and a big, thick body. Thomas is not any of those things. Plus, he looks like he's barely old enough to be here.

I can't help laughing, though, and I look at him skeptically. "Do I really look like a Katherine?"

He tilts his head to the side as if really considering my question. "Nope, not Katherine. Rachel?"

I blow out a breath. What am I doing? Well, I know what I want to be doing, but it's not looking good. When I delivered cupcakes to Violet at Red's Diner today, she invited me and the rest of the girls from Sugar Glaze to come out tonight. Violet's husband is the running back for the Jasper Eagles. Their season ended, and they were all coming out to get together before some of their teammates leave to go out of town. I guess the team doesn't get back together for training until spring, so they'll have a few months off.

When she invited me, I knew I had to come. First of all, it's in Jasper, which is thirty minutes away from our small town of Whiskey Run. And I'm not cutting on my small hometown, but the picking for men is dwindling fast. Plus, for what I have in mind, it's better here in Jasper. If I wanted a man, a white picket fence, and two point five kids, I'd be fine in Whiskey Run. But I don't want forever. No, I'm just looking for one night. I just want to blow off some steam and then I'll be back to my regular, independent self. And I can't do that in Whiskey Run without the whole town knowing about it.

"Not Rachel either," I mutter, looking around the bar. It's filling up fast, and I'm pretty sure it's because word has gotten around that players from the Jasper Eagles are going to be here. I'm looking for Violet or even her husband, Josh. He'd be easy to spot because I'm sure there would be a crowd around him. Too bad Emery, Becca, and Tara didn't come with me. We all work at the bakery together, and we spend a lot of time together outside of work. Emery had a date tonight, but I don't know why she even bothers. Every one she goes on, she finds something wrong with the guy. I think she's still hooked on her ex-husband, even though she denies it. And then Becca was at home, refusing to go out. She's still recovering from her breakup with the two-timer, and even though the other girls and I agreed to give her time, I think her time is almost up. She needs to get back out there. And then Tara had plans with her new boyfriend.

"Jennifer?" Thomas asks, leaning across the table.

I lean back. "Nope. Not Jennifer either. I'm sorry, Thomas, but really, my boyfriend should be here any minute."

He doesn't believe me. It's obvious he doesn't by the way his eyes widen and he stares at me without blinking. I don't give myself away, though. I keep my face unguarded and smile at him. Damn, I really don't want to hurt his feelings, but he's not taking a hint at all.

"Okay, well, I'll just hang out here and make sure you're okay until he gets here. I'll keep you safe."

I start to stutter. "Thank you but..." My phone starts to ring, and Violet's picture shows up on the caller ID. "Sorry, I need to get this," I tell Thomas and put the phone up to my ear.

"Hey, Vi!" I answer.

"Ugh, don't kill me..."

"What's wrong?" I ask her as Thomas perks up next to me.

"Our babysitter fell through. I'm so sorry, April."

I'm bummed, but I don't want her to feel guilty. "No, don't apologize, I completely understand. Really, I promise."

"Look, I'm going to have Josh call his friend that is going to be there and he's going to find you and make sure you make it out to your car safely, so stay put, don't move."

"No, that's not necessary. I'm fine."

"No!" she all but screams into the phone.

I don't know if it's because the noise in the background here or what, but it seems really important to her that I don't move. "Violet, this is Jasper..."

She interrupts me before I can get it all out. "Yeah, and it's not safe. Just do this for me. Okay?"

I roll my eyes even though I'm not really mad about it. This is how Violet is. She tries to take care of everybody. "Fine. I'll stay put."

Thomas smiles and nods his head. I know he can't hear Violet on the phone, but he can hear what I'm saying. Grrr, I'm going to have to be rude and ask him to leave me alone.

"I really am sorry, April. I hate that you drove all the way there. I promise I'll make it up to you."

"It's fine. Really. I completely understand. These things happen," I tell her, and before I can hang up, she asks me, "What are you wearing?"

Oh my goodness, are we really doing this? I think. Surely I can walk the thirty steps from the door to my car. But I know Violet, and I know there's no sense in arguing with her. "Yellow shirt." I look around the almost full bar. "Honestly, I think I'm the only one not wearing black. Was there a theme?"

She snorts into the phone. "No, there wasn't a theme."

I nod, looking around. Seriously, almost everyone is wearing black or dark clothing. I know it's slimming or whatever, but I guess I don't worry about things like that. I have curves, and I've learned to love them.

"Okay, I'll talk to you later," Violet says before hanging up the phone.

I barely get it into my pocket and Thomas says excitedly with a snap of his fingers, "Cassie?"

I grunt and shake my head. "No, not Cassie. Really, Thomas, my boyfriend will be here any minute, and he probably won't like me talking to someone else."

He shrugs like it's not a big deal, and all I can think is he doesn't believe me. He doesn't believe I have a boyfriend. Maybe I'm not very convincing, I don't know, but instead of arguing with him, I sit here and let him keep guessing my name. I mean, it could be worse. Even though he is too young for me, at least he's nice.

Chapter 2

Matt

I'm at the front entrance of the bar when my cell phone starts to ring. I step out of the line of people going in and stop next to the door. It's Josh's name on the caller ID. "Hey, bud, I'm about to walk in."

"I need a favor," he starts.

I don't even hesitate. I was new to the Jasper Eagles this season, and Josh was the first one to welcome me and to help me fit in with the rest of the team. If he needs something, I'll do it. No problem. "Sure thing, what's up?"

"Our babysitter cancelled on us, and we won't make it...."

I raise my hand even though he can't see me. "Well, maybe I should have asked first. I mean, you know I love kids, but I'm not sure if I'd be the best babysitter," I tell him honestly.

He starts to laugh. "Ha! I don't need you to babysit. Look, Violet invited one of her friends to meet us at the bar, and we feel bad just leaving her there. Do you care to make sure she gets out to her car safely?"

"Oh yeah, no problem. How do I find her?" I ask as I stare through the front window of the bar. Instantly, my eyes are drawn to a woman in yellow. Unfortunately, she's sitting with a man, but it doesn't stop me from staring at her. Even though her lower half is hidden behind the table, I can tell she's exactly my type of woman. Her long black hair is pulled up in a high ponytail that curls down her back. Her curvy body has my heart racing, and without realizing it, I put my hand up to my chest as if I can calm it or something.

"Hey, Matt. Earth to Matt. You still there?"

I clench my jaw and watch as the woman laughs and rolls her eyes at the man she's sitting with. "Yeah, I'm still here," I answer him without taking my eyes off the woman.

"So you think you can find her?" he asks.

"Sorry, I blanked out there for a minute. It's pretty busy here. How did you say I could find her?"

"Violet says she's wearing yellow."

I gulp. "Yellow?"

"Yep, that's what she said."

I force my eyes off the woman in yellow and do a quick scan of the bar. She's definitely the only woman in yellow. "She doesn't have a boyfriend or anything?"

I hear him ask Violet. "No, no boyfriend. So you think you can find her?"

"What's her name?" I ask.

"April."

"Yeah, brother. I can find her. Don't worry, I'll take care of her," I tell him before hanging up. I step back into line at the entrance. I know I could bypass it, but I'm not that guy. As soon as I get to the door, I make a beeline for the woman in yellow and don't stop until I'm hovering next to her at the table.

I put my hand on her shoulder, because how could I not touch her? "April."

She looks up at me, and a mixture of reactions cross her face. Surprise, attraction, and then relief. She quickly looks away and at the man sitting across from her. "See, here's my boyfriend now," she says to him, gesturing to me. Her hand goes to mine that is still fitted on her shoulder.

The man is staring at me open-mouthed before

closing it and looking at April. "Your boyfriend is Matt Adams? Center for the Jasper Eagles?"

She opens her mouth in surprise, and all I can think is what a perfect opportunity to kiss her. I lean down and press my lips to hers. She gasps, and because I can't resist, I swipe my tongue across her lower lip. She moans, and I force myself to pull away. I look into her eyes, and she's looking back at me with shock. Fuck, I just met her. Hell, I haven't really even met her yet, and already I'm manhandling her. I pull back and try to keep my cool. I reach my hand out to the other man. "Yeah, I'm Matt. It's nice to meet you."

The man starts to stutter. "She said she had a boyfriend, but I had no idea. I'm sorry," he says, looking between me and April.

I look at her, wondering what he has to say sorry for. Do I need to take care of this or what? Did he disrespect her?

April shakes her head. "No, really, it's fine. I appreciate you keeping me company. It was nice meeting you, Thomas."

He nods and gets up to leave but stops quickly. "Uh, do you think? I mean… would it be okay?"

He's looking at me, and I know where this is going even though it's taking a while to get it out.

"What is it, Thomas?" I ask him, urging him to spit it out. I'm never rude. At least I try not to be, but my patience is running thin. I want to talk to April... alone.

"Can I get a picture with you?"

"Sure." I squeeze April's shoulder before letting it go. I move around to the other side of the table, and Thomas is holding his phone up to get the selfie. He's quite a bit shorter than me, and his hand is shaking, so I take the phone and snap a few selfies of us real quick before handing him the phone back. "There you go. It was nice meeting you. Thanks for looking out for my girl," I tell him, but the whole time my eyes are on April.

She's watching me, and her eyes widen when I call her my girl. *That's right, sweetness. You're going to be mine.*

Thomas walks away, staring at the pictures on his phone, and I sit down in the chair he vacated. "Hey, April."

She takes a deep breath. "Hey."

I slide my chair around the table to get closer to her. "It's loud in here, huh?"

She nods, and I can't take my eyes off her. She's beautiful, and I know I can't fuck this up. I reach my hand across the table between us. "I guess I should formally introduce myself. I'm Matt."

She looks at my outstretched hand for just a minute before finally putting hers in it. I should shake it and let it go, but I don't. I hold on to it, stroking my thumb across her wrists. Her skin is soft against mine.

"I'm April," she says.

"Josh asked me to check in on you," I explain.

Instantly she pulls her hand back. "Oh right, you were going to make sure I made it to my car safely. But I promise it wasn't my idea. I can make it to my car. I know you have a party to get to, so I'll..."

She's rambling, and when she stands up as if she's going to leave, I stand up too. "Wait."

She stops but doesn't sit back down. "Hear me out? Hang out for a minute. I'm not in any rush."

Her eyes are telling me she wants to, but she shakes her head. "No, I don't want to keep you."

I reach for her, tugging her to me. She lets her body melt to mine, and my first thought is she's going to know exactly what I'm thinking because there's no hiding my desire for her. Not after feeling her curvy, thick body against mine. "You're not. Come on, have a drink with me before you go."

She knows. Her hips press against mine, and

her lips tilt up in a smile that is not meant to seduce, but that's exactly what it does. She has me hook, line, and sinker. "Okay, I can stay for a little while."

I nod and reach for her chair, holding it until she sits down. I pull mine closer and sit down with my thighs open and her legs between mine. "Tell me about you."

She shrugs her shoulders. "I'm April. I'm a baker at Sugar Glaze Bakery in Whiskey Run."

I lean closer and inhale. "Is that why you smell so sweet?"

She laughs and playfully swats at my chest. I catch her hand because it's an excuse to touch her. I need to touch her. "I'm serious. You smell really good."

She swallows. "Uh, actually, I joke about that all the time. I sometimes feel like I've got sugar baked into my skin. I am always smelling sugar and vanilla even when I'm not at work."

I press my nose to the side of her neck. She doesn't resist me. Her head tilts to the other side, and I feel her body tremble against me when I touch my lips behind her ear.

I pull back and shift in my seat. "Yeah, sugar and vanilla."

Her eyes are wide. "So what about you? What's a center?" she asks.

I try to hide my smirk. So she doesn't follow football. "Uh a center is the one that hikes the ball."

She looks at my hand on hers. I'm tracing on the back of her hand, and I switch up directions because I realize I'm drawing hearts on her. She scrunches her nose up. "Hikes it?"

I could brag and tell her that the center pretty much is the leader of the offensive line, but I don't want to sound conceited. "Yeah, to the quarterback."

She nods. "Cool. I'll have to watch a game now and see you hike your ball."

Her face turns red, but all I can think about is having her watch me. I'd love that. I'd love to have her cheering for me from the sidelines. "I'd like that. But we don't play again until spring."

She doesn't commit. She even rears back a little when I mention the timeframe, letting me know she's skittish. I lay my hand firmly across hers either to hold her to me or to calm her, I'm not sure. How in the world have Josh and Violet kept this woman a secret? I can already imagine if my teammates knew about her, they would have already made a play for her. Which brings me to my next question. "How do you know Josh and Violet?"

Chapter 3

April

His hand on mine is driving me crazy. He's a big guy, making me feel small and almost dainty next to him. I snap my eyes up to his, and he's still looking at me with his big, brown, soulful eyes. "I'm sorry, what?" I ask.

He leans in because I guess he thought I couldn't hear him. "How do you know Josh and Violet?"

I turn my head, but instead of his ear, I'm looking straight at him, our faces so close I can feel his breath on my cheek. "Uh, you know Violet owns Red's Diner in Whiskey Run?"

He nods, staring at my lips. "Yeah, I knew she owned a diner."

"Well, her diner is just down the street from the

bakery, and well, have you ever been to Whiskey Run?"

He shakes his head. "Nope. I know it's only thirty minutes from here, but I haven't been there."

"Well, it's a small town, and we all know each other, but Violet is a good friend of mine. I make cupcakes for her to sell in the diner, and we sort of hit it off from the start."

"I want to try one of your cupcakes," he says with a lick of his lips.

I laugh. "Well, the next time you're in Whiskey Run, you'll have to come by the bakery or the diner and grab one."

He clears his throat and sits back. "I'm here for another week... less than a week actually."

"Oh, you don't live here in Jasper?"

"I have an apartment here during the season, but I planned to go home until spring," he says, and I swear he almost looks sad about it.

"Where's home?" I ask him.

A waitress comes to stand next to our table. She's staring at Matt, but he doesn't seem to notice. "Can I get you all anything?"

He looks at me with raised eyebrows, and I shake my head. "No, thanks."

"Are you sure?" he asks.

"No really. I have to drive. I'm good," I tell him.

"Nothing, thank you," he tells the waitress, still looking at me. She looks almost longingly at him before walking away.

"So where's home?" I ask him again.

"Texas," he says.

An idea forms in my head. "And you're only here for a week?" I ask to be sure I heard him right.

He nods, searching my face. He wants to say something. He opens his mouth but then closes it quickly.

I'm about to ask him what he wants to say when someone comes up to him and slaps him on the back. "Hey, Matt! They have a private room in the back. That's where the party's at."

Matt looks up at him, and it's obviously one of his teammates. He's built like a football player anyway. "Hey, yeah, I'll be there in a minute."

The guy looks between Matt and me before leaning around Matt toward me. He holds out his hand. "Hey, I'm James."

Matt's hand that is on mine tightens, so I lift my other hand. "Hi. I'm April."

James starts to lift my hand to his mouth, and before I can tug it away, Matt stands up, forcing James to step back and drop my hand. He turns to his friend. "Go ahead, James. I'll be back there in a minute."

James wants to argue with him. It's obvious by the crease of his forehead he doesn't like to be told what to do. But thankfully, he just nods at Matt. "See you around, April."

I don't answer him because he's already walking toward the back.

Matt takes a deep breath as he hovers over me. There's indecision on his face, and I wait to see what he's thinking.

"So I have to go say hi at least. Want to go with me?"

"Uh, I don't think so," I answer instantly.

"Are you sure? I won't leave your side," he says.

But I shake my head.

He looks toward the back and then at me. "Okay, so will you wait for me? Literally, ten minutes. Probably less."

I go to stand up. "I can just go. I don't want you missing your party…"

He puts his hands on my shoulders. "No, really, I just need to make an appearance. In and out." He pushes a piece of hair away from my face and tucks it behind my ear. "Plus, I want to spend some time with you."

My body shudders because he's saying exactly what I'm feeling. I want to spend some time with him too. "Are you sure?" I ask him.

He leans in, and I think he's going to kiss me again. The first one was unexpected, but damn, it was good. When his lips press to my forehead, I sigh because I may have wanted his lips on mine, but this is just sweet. How can he look like he does and be gentle and sweet? I ignore the pounding of my heart in my chest. "I'll be right here."

He watches me as I sit down, and when he makes no move to go, I can't help but laugh. I've never felt a pull of attraction like this. "The sooner you go, the sooner you can get back," I tell him.

That seems to wake him up. "Right. Right. I'll be right back. Don't move," he says, and only when I agree does he walk away, practically jogging to the back.

I watch him until I can't see him anymore and then look around the bar. There are people everywhere, laughing and having a good time. I pick up my phone and see I missed a text from Violet. She was asking if I made it home safe.

I text her back. "Not yet. Can I call you?"

I wait for her to text back. Normally, I'd just call

her, but I don't know if JJ is asleep or what, and I don't want to wake him up.

I practically jump out of my skin as I'm staring at the phone and it starts to ring. I laugh and put it up to my ear. "What's wrong? Are you okay?" Violet says.

"Yes, I'm fine. I'm sorry. I didn't mean to worry you. I just had a question, that's all."

"Sheeeew. I was worried for a minute. Sure, what's up?"

I put my hand to my head. I probably should have thought about this a little more. "So uh, what can you tell me about Matt Adams?"

She's silent for a second, and I'm beginning to think she didn't hear me. "You know, the center for Josh's team."

She laughs at that, and I mean loud. I have to pull my phone away from my ear. "Oh, you know football now? That's hilarious."

"Har, har. Seriously, what do you know about him?"

"Well, Josh likes him. He seems like a good guy. Always real polite to me. He has a good reputation. Doesn't party, or at least if he does, it's not all over the news or anything."

"Okay," I say, lost in thought.

"Okay? What does that even mean?" she asks me.

"It means I think I found the one."

"What? April, that's so great. I'm so happy for you—" she starts, but I interrupt her when I realize she has the wrong idea. "No, not the one the one. I mean, remember us talking earlier today and me telling you that I just needed a one-night stand? Well, he's perfect. He's leaving this week. He's a good guy. And I mean, damn, he's hot."

"Wait. He's leaving?" she asks. "I didn't know he was leaving."

"Yeah, but he'll be back in spring for football. This is perfect."

She sounds hesitant. "If you're sure this is what you want...."

"I am," I tell her. I've had relationships before, and they were always disappointing. I don't need a man that's more interested in hanging out with his friends than me. Heck, I lost count of how many times my ex, Reagan, left me at home and went to a party or whatever. I definitely don't need that in my life. But I do miss the intimacy, which is how I came up with this plan."

We're mid conversation when a man stands next

to me. "Hey, Violet, I have to go. I'll call you tomorrow," I tell her before hanging up.

"Hello."

He reaches for the chair next to me. "So what's a pretty thing like you doing here by yourself? Mind if I have a seat?"

He's about to sit down when Matt reappears. He leans over me with a big smile on his face. He kisses me, and this time, I put my hands on each side of his neck to hold him there. His muscles bunch under my palms, and he deepens the kiss. There's a shrill scream and then laughter across the room that has me pulling back. "Wow," he says at the same time I do.

The man that was going to sit down is long gone, and Matt sits in the seat next to mine. "That didn't take long. I promise if you want to go—I mean, you all are here to celebrate, right?"

He shrugs like he could care less. "I can celebrate with you."

That's my opening, and before I can talk myself out of it, I blurt out, "Would you like to come to my house tonight?"

He's up, pulling me into his arms in an instant. "Yes. I would love to."

Standing up next to him as he holds me against

him, feeling his body pressed to mine makes me think that we fit perfectly together. "Great. Let's get out of here," I say breathlessly.

His arm goes around my waist, and we walk outside. The whole way, I'm chanting to myself, *One night, one night, one night.*

Chapter 4

Matt

"Where's your car parked?" I ask her.

She points to the side lot, and we start to walk that way. The farther we get from the bar, the tenser she gets. A fear like nothing I've ever felt starts to come over me. I've faced three hundred and fifty pound linemen that would have liked nothing more than to put me flat on my back, but nothing compares to the fear of April changing her mind and walking away from me.

"Are you okay?" I ask her as she stops next to a red VW convertible bug.

She shrugs. "Yeah, it's just..."

I put my finger under her chin and lift so she's looking at me. "What is it?"

She blinks her big green eyes at me. "I just..." She takes a deep breath and blows it out. "I just don't want you to think I do this all the time. I've never met someone and just... well, you know. I guess I don't want you to think badly of me."

"I don't. And me either. I've never met a woman at a bar and gone home with her. So this is new for both of us... but I don't want this night to be over. Not yet."

For that, she smiles, and I swear it lights up the whole damn parking lot. "Me either."

I force my breathing to calm and then pull my phone from my pocket. "What's your phone number?"

She recites it, and I punch the numbers into my phone and save her in my contacts. As I open her car door, I start to talk. "I know Whiskey Run is around thirty minutes away, and that's a long time to think. You can change your mind about what happens when we get there, but I don't want you changing your mind about spending time with me, okay?"

"Okay," she answers and looks at me with relief.

I help her into the car, steal a quick kiss, and then call her phone. She laughs when it rings, but at least she plays along. "Hello?"

I shut her door and take a step back. "Put me on speaker."

She does what I ask and then lays her phone in the cup holder. "I'm going to talk to you the whole way home."

Her face lights up. "Okay."

I turn to go and walk across the parking lot to my truck, talking to her the whole way. I get in, turn the ignition, and connect my phone to the speakers. "Are you there?" I ask her as I set my phone down.

"Yeah, I'm here." I can hear the smile on her face. She stops next to me, waves, and then drives on. I pull out quickly, not wanting to let her out of my sight.

"So tell me about you."

"What do you want to know?"

I follow closely behind her. "Anything.... everything."

Her soft laugh sounds as if it's fluttering through the speakers. "Okay, we'll start easy. Favorite color?"

"Pink. What's your favorite color?"

If she'd asked me earlier, I'd have said blue, but now it's green. "Green. And not green like the grass, green like your eyes, the color of emeralds."

She gasps and starts to laugh again. "You're smooth. I'll give you that."

I shake my head even though she can't see it. "I'm not, though. Ask anyone. I have no game... I'm definitely not a player."

She whistles softly. "I don't know, you have something going for you. I mean, I did ask you to come over."

I shift in my seat, trying to let some pressure off my cock expanding in my jeans. I clear my throat, but my voice still sounds husky. "What else? What's your favorite food? Do you like to read or watch TV? What do you do in your spare time?"

She laughs, and for the next twenty minutes, we go back and forth and get to know one another. We discover that we have a lot in common. She loves to cook, and I love to eat. Her parents have been married for over thirty years, and so have mine. And we both enjoy watching anything that is funny.

When we get to the sign letting us know we've reached Whiskey Run, I lean forward in my seat. We're close, and it's like my body realizes it. The whole way, listening to her talk, I've had a tremble in my hand. A need to touch her, and it won't be much longer. "Okay, we're in the infamous town of Whiskey Run. Tell me about it."

She starts pointing out different landmarks, and I

quickly realize we're driving through downtown. "Right up here on the left is Red's Diner."

I look to the left and see the sign. "So we're close to the bakery?"

"Yep, it's on the right. See? Right there. Sugar Glaze."

"I see it," I tell her as I look at the big sign with the pink cupcake and flashing neon sign. We drive a few more blocks, and she points out a bar, a tattoo shop, the library, and an auto repair shop.

We get just a few blocks, and she puts on her signal. "This is me."

I follow behind her and watch as she pulls into a little yellow house with a big porch. She stops her car, and I park my truck right behind her.

She's fidgeting on the sidewalk when I get next to her. "Hey."

She smiles and looks at me under her long lashes. "Hey. Come on in."

I walk behind her, watching her hips sway back and forth. I put my hands in the front pockets of my jeans to resist reaching for her. She has the door unlocked, and we're inside before she takes a deep breath and looks at me. "Gah, I'm nervous. I didn't think I'd be this nervous."

"Don't be nervous. Just relax."

She nods. "Okay, do you want to sit down?"

I follow her into the living room, taking in all the photos on the wall. She sits down, so I sit next to her and immediately she pops up. "Are you hungry? Do you want something to eat?"

Without thinking, I stand next to her and put my hands on her hips. "Are you on the menu?"

She turns in my arms and stares up at me. It may possibly kill me if she changes her mind, but I don't want to fuck this up. She wants to wait, I'll wait. It doesn't matter now. I can sit on this couch the rest of the night with her in my arms. I may be uncomfortable and have blue balls by morning, but I'll do it.

She's watching me closely, and I lean in and kiss her on her forehead. She presses into me, and I try to ignore the way my body reacts to having her this close. But she doesn't. I know she feels it by the way her hips press against mine. I go to move my hips back. "Sorry. I want you, April."

Her hands go to my hips to hold me still. "You do, don't you?"

I laugh huskily. "Yeah, honey. There's no hiding it."

She presses her lips to my chest. The thin

material of my T-shirt is between us, and I don't want that. I don't want anything between us.

I cup her face and tilt it up. She licks her lower lip, and I don't even try to resist. I press my mouth to hers, and it's an immediate frenzy. It's as if I've pounced on her because before I realize it. I've walked her backwards until her back is pressed against the wall and I'm fitted against her head to toe. She grunts when her back hits the wall, and I try to pull away to ask if her if she's okay, but she doesn't let me.

Her hands are everywhere. Spanning my shoulders, down my chest, around my waist and then her nails are digging into my back, up and down until I'm groaning against her.

I nudge her head to the side and trail kisses along her neck and down the V of her T-shirt. She's breathing heavily, and I pull at the hem of her shirt. She raises her arms, and I pull the cloth off her body quickly. Her nipples are hard and pressed against her bra. I fit my mouth over top of the material, and she whimpers. It's not enough.

She must feel the same because she reaches behind her back and unclasps her bra, letting it fall down her shoulders and to the floor. I moan, seeing this part of her. She's beautiful and perfect. I cup her, flicking my thumb along her nipple and then putting my mouth on her again. With each suckle, she raises higher on her toes, making little pleasure noises.

I lift away just enough to ask, "Where's your bed?"

She doesn't mutter a word. She grabs my hand, and I follow her down the hall and into her bedroom. She turns on the light, which I find hot as fuck. I thought I'd have to convince her to leave a light on because I want to see her. Every fuckin' inch.

She stops next to the bed, and when she turns, I want to lay her back and feast on her, but she has ideas of her own. She drops to her knees onto the carpeted floor. I take off my shirt, and she watches me, taking it all in. Her hands are at my waist, and she undoes my pants. I work on kicking off my shoes, and she pulls my pants and underwear down in one quick swoop.

My cock is standing straight up, begging for attention. She leans in, her eyes on mine as she sticks her tongue out and licks the drop of precum off the tip of my cock. My hips jerk, and I know in this instant that my life will never be the same. I've never felt anything or reacted to a woman like this... April's special, and I can't fuck this up.

I wrap my hand in her ponytail and tilt her head up. I push my hips back and lean down, hovering my mouth over hers. "You keep that up, and I'm going to come."

She licks her lips. "Isn't that the point?"

I smile at her. "Yeah, but not yet. When I come, I want to do it with the taste of you on my tongue."

She presses her lips to mine and pops off quickly. "There you go."

I shake my head, looking into her eyes. "No, honey. I want to taste your pussy."

I pull her up and lay her back on the bed, undoing her pants and pulling them down in one fluid motion. I climb up the mattress, moving my wide shoulders between her legs. Her cunt is already glistening for me, as if it's begging to be feasted on.

I don't hesitate. I press my lips to hers in a gentle kiss and then swipe my tongue through her wet, swollen slit. Her hips raise, and I use one of my arms to hold them down. She tastes as sweet as a lollipop. One taste and I can't stop. I latch on to her swollen clit, and she moans as I apply more pressure. Heavy then soft, heavy then soft. She tries to roll her hips, and I smile against her. She's already so damn close.

Gently, I push a finger inside her. She's tight, and I hook my finger, searching for the special spot that's going to have her coming like a rocket. With my tongue on her clit and my finger massaging her G-spot, she moans and starts to writhe underneath me. I don't stop until her whole body pulls taut, and her hips automatically start to ride against my face. I eat it all up, lapping at the fresh cream.

I'm hard as a pipe and ready to blow. I want nothing more than to enter her bare and consequences be damned, but she's too far gone to make that kind of a decision. "You have a condom?"

A part of me hopes she says no, but she lifts her head and points at the table next to the bed. "Top drawer. I, uh, don't normally just have them. I mean, I bought them for tonight."

I grab the box of condoms and tear the box apart to open them. I'm ripping the package open and sliding it on my hard dick when I realize what she said. "You knew you'd be having sex tonight?"

I should delve into that question or at least wait for an answer, but I'm not thinking clearly right now. I need to come, and I need to be inside her when I do.

She leans up on her elbows. "That sounds awful, but can we talk about it later?"

I'm already lining up at her entrance, slowly moving inside her. She's tight, and the aftermath of her orgasm made her slick, but the tiny vibrations are beating against me, and fuck, it feels good. When I'm balls deep, a groan from low in my chest comes out, and I swear I want to bang my fist on my chest like a fuckin' caveman. I've never felt pussy this good.

Chapter 5

April

I've never felt anything this good. Matt definitely knows what he's doing. My neighbors probably hear the groan he practically screamed a second ago, but I don't care. There's something possessive and earth-shattering about knowing that I can do that to him. That I can make him feel like that.

"You okay?" he asks me.

I could say something smart or even something about the size of his dick. He's big, and the size of it scared me a little. But I should have known. The rest of him is big.

"Yeah, I'm good."

He pushes his hips into me, and I groan.

"Are you sure—" he starts to ask me, but I interrupt him. "Move."

He doesn't wait. His hips start to move. He slides in and out of me, angling his hips so he's hitting my already sensitive G-spot. Over and over, the friction becomes too much, and I'm about to come again. He knows it too. My legs tighten on his hips.

"Fuck, you're so wet... so hot."

"Kiss me," I all but beg him.

He leans over, his cock pummeling in and out of me, and presses his lips to mine. I can taste myself on him, and we both groan. Every sense is electrified, and I moan as another orgasm races through my body. I feel it everywhere, and it's so intense, I jerk and writhe, pushing him away and then pulling him back. It's too much.

"Arrrgh!" he screams against my mouth as his already rock-hard body gets even harder. He comes, his body jerking out of control, and we ride the wave of complete and utter satisfaction.

I'm spent. Completely spent. I don't even know if I can move at this point. He's rested his body on mine, and when he starts to pull away, saying he's too heavy, I hold him to me, not letting him go. I know this is one night, and I'm not ready for it to end. He'll probably leave, so if I can drag it out just a little bit more, commit the feeling of him, the smell of him, the taste of him to memory, then that's what I'm going to do.

He doesn't seem to mind this possessive hold I have on him. He's kissing me softly and starts to rise again. I let him go this time, and his voice is gruff. "I'll be right back."

He stands up and stretches. "Where's the bathroom?"

I point to the door next to my open closet. "There."

He goes in, and I stretch, already feeling the soreness in the muscles I haven't used in a while.

He's back within minutes, his still impressive cock hanging between his legs. He stops next to the bed and leans over me. He kisses me first, and then I feel the warmth of a wet cloth between my legs as he cleans me up. Damn, this man is going to spoil me.

He's gone again and back. I expect him to dress and put his boots on, but he doesn't. He lies down next to me, pulling my body against his.

We're both quiet, and the longer that nothing is said, the more I feel like I need to explain.

"I bought those earlier today because I was planning on sleeping with someone tonight."

His body tautens against mine. "Did you have a date or something?"

I roll my eyes. Gah, this is going to sound awful. "No, I planned on having a one-night stand. I went out tonight wanting to..."

He holds his hand up. "I get the picture... why?"

This time I don't keep it in. I groan. "Ugh, do we really need to talk about this?"

He holds me tighter. "I'm not judging... I'm just curious."

I lean my head down and lay it on his chest. The light is still on, and this is going to be so much easier having this discussion if I don't have to look at him. "I broke up with my ex six months ago. He was a bit of an ass. He was interested in me... when we were by ourselves. When it was just the two of us, it was perfect. Any other time... well, it wasn't."

He kisses the top of my head. "Why not? What did he do?"

I clench my eyes, hating to think about this again. "Well, it took me a while to figure it out, but he was ashamed of me. He loved my plus-size body, but I guess he didn't want other people to know he did. If we went places, he ignored me. A lot of people didn't even know we were dating." I take a deep breath. "Anyway, I decided I deserved more. I'm fine with who I am. I like my body just the way it is, so I broke up with him and swore I wasn't going to get involved again. Not with someone like him."

"And?"

I sigh. "And, well, this is where I sound like a tramp. I missed it. I missed being intimate with someone. So I went out planning to have a one-night stand."

He's quiet, and I'm sure he's going to get up any second and take off running. This is way too deep for a first date. Fuck, this isn't even a date. This is a one-night stand.

"He's a dumbass, April. Any man that would hide you... fuck, he ain't it. He ain't worthy. I'm glad you left him. I'm glad you went out tonight, and I'm glad I'm the lucky son of a bitch that found you. When I saw you through the window, even before I knew who you were, I wanted you."

I smack him on the chest, and he catches it, bringing my palm up to his lips. He kisses my palm. "I mean it, April."

Speechless, I lie there in wonder. He thinks he's the lucky one. I'm the lucky one. Emotion wrecks through my senses, and I can't speak, so I turn and press my lips to his bare chest, right over his heart. We lie there for the longest time with his heart beating under my cheek and his hand stroking through my hair.

Chapter 6

Matt

One night. All she wants is one night, and I'm already trying to figure out how to see her again.

I hate hearing about her ex. Not only because of the way he treated her but because of the fact I don't want to think about her with someone else. She's mine and has been since I first laid eyes on her. But obviously, I can't tell her that. I have a feeling she'd freak if I even hinted at that.

Her breathing starts to even out, and I know she's asleep. She pushes into me, burying herself deeper against me, and I hold her tighter.

I fight sleep. If I sleep, I'm going to miss how it feels with her in my arms. Since her confession, I've felt a sense of unease and foreboding. I understand her theory and why she thought she wanted only one night, but I'm going to prove her wrong. I'm going to prove to her that I'm exactly what she wants and needs.

My mind is going crazy. It's like everything is whirling in there at once. I'm thinking of April and the feel of her body against mine. I take a breath, and her scent has my cock hardening again already. And it's outrageous, but I'm trying to figure out what to do. I'm supposed to go back home to Texas later this week. I need to see my family, who I haven't gotten to spend a lot of time with since I was traded to the Eagles. But can I really leave and not see April again until spring? No fuckin' way.

Questions start to form in my head. Should I stay in my apartment in Jasper until spring season? Should I find something in Whiskey Run? Should I wake her up and tell her what I'm thinking? I lean my head down and kiss the top of her head. Definitely not. She'll think I'm crazy and probably kick me out of here.

No, I need to handle this one day at a time.

It's hours later, and I feel as if I've just fallen asleep when she jostles next to me. We're facing each other, still naked, and my cock is hard, pressed against her belly.

She looks so sweet, and the small smile on her face tells me she's satisfied or dreaming of something nice. I hope it's about me.

I'm waxing all poetic, and that's not me. That's not who I am. Fuck, the guys would have a field day if they saw this softer side of me. I'm supposed to be tough, and up until this very moment I would have said I'm the toughest offensive lineman in the league. Just don't get me started on April because once I do, I can feel the guard I have on my heart softening, and for the first time, I want someone to see me for me. Not the tough guy, not the pro football player, and not the rich guy with endorsements. I want her to see me as the man I am. A man that was raised by a single mom and has worked his whole life to get where he's at. A man that protects his family and his friends no matter what. And a man that has been lost, searching for something and who is pretty sure he's found it—or her—tonight.

April stirs next to me, and her groggy voice fills the darkness. "Matt?"

She's reaching out like she's searching for me, and I don't even try to contain my smile. "Yeah, baby. I'm right here."

"Are you leaving?" she asks.

I want to ask her if she wants me to, but I'm afraid of the answer. "No, I'm not leaving."

She sighs, and maybe it's me being hopeful, but she seems happy with my answer. "Okay."

I slide my hand down her back and cup her naked ass. She lifts her leg and lays it over mine, getting us closer. All I have to do is move her up a little bit and I can have her again. The thought penetrates my mind until I'm as hard as a rock. She feels it, and I'm about to lift away when she raises up and smiles at me. The only light is the moonlight streaming through the half-closed curtains. Instead of moving her up, she slides down my body, and I suck in a breath. Fuck, my lower body jerks as she comes to rest between my legs. She hovers over me, and when her pink tongue comes out and touches the tip of my penis, I let out a guttural groan. She takes me deep into her mouth until I hit the back of her throat. "Aaaaah!" I moan. She cups my balls as she slides her tongue up and down the length of me. She moves, moaning around my shaft, making my lower belly pull. I won't last.

I touch the back of her neck. She slows down but doesn't stop.

"April," I say huskily.

She looks up at me, and it takes everything I have

not to come right then. Her eyes on me with my dick in her mouth is going to be my kryptonite. My hips jerk. "Honey, I'm going to come."

She moans but doesn't lift off. She doesn't look like she wants to, either. She keeps taking me, deeper and deeper, and finally I can't hold back. She finishes me as my hips jerk erratically, shooting my cum down her throat. She takes it all, licking her lips when she pops off her lips with a smack.

She climbs up my body and snuggles against my chest. A part of me was afraid she'd be back in the mode of the one-night nonsense and try to kick me out the door, but she hasn't yet. I cup her ass, bringing her against me tighter. "I swear I almost blacked out there for a minute. I just need to recover a little and then I'm going to take care of you."

"No way, we're even now," she says and then yawns.

I pull away a little to look down at her face on my chest. "Even? What do you mean even?"

"I mean I came twice earlier. Now we're even."

My forehead creases. I don't know if I like this logic. I don't want to be even. Does she think this is a game and I'm keeping count? Making sure I'm getting mine before I go? Fuck that. This is definitely not a game to me.

I push her until she's lying on her back and I'm hovering over her. Her eyes round, and she gasps as I lower my body over hers. She's looking up at me, and I tell her exactly what I'm thinking. "Your logic is a little fucked up."

She smirks. "How so?"

"Because when you get yours... I get mine. You think the taste of your pussy on my lips isn't doing something for me? Because it is... I put my lips on you, my tongue on you, or my dick in you... I'm getting mine too. But yeah, honey, you wanna think you owe me? That's fine... I'll take it."

Her smile is instantaneous, and I can't resist showing her exactly what having her on my tongue does for me.

Chapter 7

April

Ring. Ring.

I hear it in the very depths of sleep. It takes me a minute, but I finally figure out it's my phone making all the racket. I jerk up just as it stops.

I push my wayward hair off my face and look at Matt. I'm a little surprised he's still here. I figured after round two last night, he would have left. But man, was I wrong. He's lying flat on his back, and as I look at him head to toe, I get caught up in the way the covers are tented at the juncture of his thighs.

I can only stare when I see it twitch. I cover my mouth so as to not to laugh.

"Getting an eyeful?" he asks, and his voice has me about to jump out of my skin. I'm caught red handed.

I'm about to laugh it off when my phone dings.

I reach over and grab it off the nightstand and see a text from Violet.

When I open it, all it has is three numbers. "911."

Instantly, I hit dial on her name and put the phone to my ear. When she answers, I immediately ask. "Violet, are you okay? What's wrong?"

I'm climbing out of bed and stumble backward, almost landing on Matt when I see he's followed me.

"No, shoot. I'm sorry, April. Nothing's wrong. I didn't mean to scare you. It's not an emergency emergency."

I put my hand over my heart and try to catch my breath. "Geez, woman, don't scare me like that."

I sit on the edge of the bed, realize I'm still naked, and blush as I look over my shoulder at Matt. He's watching me, and when he sees I'm okay, he looks at my body. His eyes darken, his nose flares, and he reaches for me. I smirk and pull the bed sheet around me. It doesn't stop him, though. He moves to my side of the bed and sits behind me, his hands on my shoulders.

I groan because it feels so good.

"What was that?" Violet asks.

Shit. I completely forgot. "Nothing. So what's up? What's the 911 that isn't an emergency?"

"Brody Andrews' son is turning three today, and the person that was baking his cake and cupcakes backed out at the last minute."

I shake my head, still foggy from being woken up and probably the lack of sleep. "Brody Andrews?"

It's like I can hear Violet roll her eyes at me. "Yes, Brody Andrews. Quarterback for the Eagles."

"Okay, what about him?"

She sighs heavily in the phone. "I know it's last minute, but they're having a birthday party for his son today. They need a small cake and approximately four dozen cupcakes."

It's Sunday. It's my day off, but I hate to turn down business. I really hate to turn down a favor for Violet. She's done so much for me through the years. "What time does it need to be there and where?"

"Three o'clock and in Jasper. I can get someone to maybe come and get them."

"It's no big deal. I can deliver them."

"I'll help," Matt says from behind me.

I turn and look at him, and he's smiling broadly.

"Wait, was that Matt?" Violet asks.

"Uh, yeah, he said he'd help get them delivered. So, uh, anyway... text me a picture of what he wants the cake to look like, any wording, and what colors. I'll get it done."

I start to hang up, and I hear Violet cackling.

I stand up, and Matt has slid to the side of the bed, puts his hands around my waist, and pulls me to his lap. "I need to shower and get to the bakery."

"I'm going to help you," he says, kissing my neck.

"Oh yeah? What are you going to help me with exactly?"

His tongue swipes from my neck to my ear. "Well, I'm thinking that I can help you get clean and then I'll go help you at the bakery."

I turn in his arms. "Really? You can bake?"

He shrugs. "I can follow directions."

I should say no. I should tell him to go and then come back to pick up the desserts at the bakery this afternoon. But I don't.

I stand up and let the sheet fall to the floor. It's like I have no inhibitions with Matt. He spent the majority of last night looking, touching, and tasting every part of me. There's no reason to hide from him now. I pull my shoulders back. "How good are you at following directions?"

His mouth falls open as he gapes at me. He must have thought he was going to have to work harder for it, but obviously the fact that I woke up next to him has me yearning for him.

He reaches for me, cupping my pussy with his

big hand. My hands go to his shoulders to steady myself, and he plunges a big, thick finger inside me. "I'll do anything you tell me to do."

He hooks his finger, rubbing against my G-spot. "Yeah, that. Do that."

He pulls me closer and licks my nipple. I groan, and my head falls back. He pulls his hand from me and stands up. He walks around me, and his hand goes to my back, pushing me until I'm bent over the bed with my ass in the air. "I love this ass," he says as he caresses me there.

His hard cock is pressed against the back of my thighs. I know I'm dripping for him. I hear him rip the wrapper, and a few seconds later, he's plunging inside me.

My forehead is on the bed and my arms are over my head. His hands are on my hips, holding me so tightly I know I'm going to have some bruises there later, but I don't even care. The feel of him inside me is everything. He's so deep, I grunt with every thrust of his hips. When he reaches around me, his finger on my swollen clit, I'm done. Two flicks and I'm thrashing my arms as my pussy sucks him in deeper. He groans as he explodes inside me. We're both panting as he pulls out of me, helping me to stand up. My legs are like Jell-O, but he doesn't let me go.

"Come on, baby. I'm going to get you clean and then we're going to the bakery so you can boss me around."

I laugh. "Oh yeah? You like that? You want me to boss you around?"

He pushes my hair out of my eyes. "If at some point you tell me to make you come again, I'll definitely like it."

My knees about buckle. I don't think I can take another round. Not yet. I can feel myself losing ground here. I don't want to make this more than it is, and the more sex—scratch that, the more he keeps making me feel like this, the more it's going to suck when it's over. I point my finger into his chest and try to hide the thoughts in my head with a smile. "Forget that, big guy. We have work to do."

He grabs my finger, kisses the end of it, and then holds my hand as we start walking to the bathroom. "You're right. We'll get clean and then go bake some cupcakes."

I stare at the back of his head, wondering if I'm even going to be able to concentrate in a kitchen with Matt. He definitely has me thinking of other things besides baking.

Chapter 8

Matt

Five hours later, I'm exhausted, but I refuse to let it show. I'm a professional athlete, but I swear working in a hot kitchen, with all the bending, cleaning, and mixing is a lot.

"You doing okay?" April asks as she finishes icing the last of the cupcakes. She's really good at what she does. And it's obvious she loves it. She's smiled the whole day, and I know she has to be exhausted too. Neither one of us got a lot of sleep last night.

I roll my eyes and lean over her. "Yes, I'm fine. I am a trained athlete. You know that, right?"

She lifts up with a smile. "Is that why I see you keep rolling your shoulders and stretching your neck?"

I grab on to my neck and massage it a little. "Old football injury. I just tweaked it."

She drops the icing bag in her hand and comes toward me. "Oh no, are you okay? Let me see."

I drop my hands and sit down on the stool so she can reach me better. She starts digging deeply into my shoulders, and I pat across my collarbone. "This too. This is hurting too."

She moves around to the front of me and starts rubbing me on the sides of my neck. I put my hands on her waist and pull her into the V of my legs. It takes her a minute, but she finally gets what I'm trying to do.

She puts her hand on my chest and pushes away. "Oh no. You have to go and get changed and take these to the party. I promised Violet they would get there on time."

I grab her hand to stop her. "You're going too."

She shakes her head and looks around at the spotless kitchen. "No, I'm not. I need to clean up."

"Try again. I already cleaned it while you were icing all those."

She blinks, trying to come up with an excuse. "I wasn't invited."

"I'm inviting you. Plus, you made the cupcakes. I mean, it's a given you're invited."

She bites her lip. "I dunno..."

I close the lid on the last box. "You're going. That's final."

I try to keep my face stern, and out of the corner of my eye, I see her pop her hip out and put her hand there. "Excuse me. You can't tell me..."

I bust out laughing, and she figures out I was playing with her. "Fine, I can't make you go. But I can ask you. Will you please go with me?" I'm afraid she's going to say no, so I tell her the only thing I can think of where there's no way she can refuse me. "I'm a bit of a klutz. What if I drop the boxes while I'm carrying them?"

"You don't carry them all at once," she says.

I play dumb and flex my arms for her. "Really? I'm pretty sure I can carry the cake and all four boxes of cupcakes at the same time. Have you seen these arms?"

She shakes her head. "Fine, you win. I'll go with you... to help set up."

"Deal," I say, leaning in to sneak a kiss.

She pulls back. "Deal? What do I get in this deal?"

I wiggle my eyebrows, and she starts walking away. "Forget it. C'mon, we gotta go if we're going to make it on time."

I load my truck up and drive us into Jasper. After a quick stop at my apartment to change clothes and to grab some more because I'm hoping that I may get another night with April, we bolt over to Brody Andrews' house.

When we get there, I leave April with Violet and Brody's wife Callie as the guys and I carry in the boxes of cupcakes.

"This is so perfect!" Callie exclaims.

I look at the dessert table and am completely amazed. April had me bring in some stands out of the truck, and she has everything displayed perfectly. The three-year-old is so excited as he stands next to his mom, jumping up and down.

April is all smiles, and I can tell she's really happy with everyone bragging on the cake and cupcakes. Little B, as Brody and Callie call their son, is thrilled with the way she made the cake look like a football field and every one of the cupcakes are designed like footballs. I saw her do it with my own eyes, but I still don't know how she did it.

Callie puts her hand on April. "Okay, so I need to know: What is the name of the bakery? Do you have any business cards?"

April nods and pats her purse. She pulls out one and hands it over. "Yeah, I have one right here."

Callie takes it. "Do you have any more?"

April's eyes widen in surprise, but she brings out more business cards. "Yeah."

Callie claps her hands together excitedly. "This is great. The moms that come will love this. The bakery we've been using has been so unreliable lately. We need someone new. Get ready; you're going to be very busy."

Callie walks over to the table and sets out the business cards before walking over to a group of moms that are admiring the table. I watch as she hands them each a card. April is speechless. Her mouth is hanging open, and she seems to get herself together when Violet draws her in for a side hug. That's the most she can do with her son JJ on her hip. I walk toward them and hear Violet ask her, "So you and Matt, huh?"

I stop mid stride, waiting to see what April is going to say when Brody and Josh holler at me from across the room. April looks up at me, wide-eyed. Dammit. I force a smile onto my face. "I'll be right back. You okay?" I ask her.

"Yeah, I'm good," she says. I can see it on her face. She's thinking about last night. Or maybe even about early this morning.

I go across the room and stop next to Josh and

Brody. "What's up?"

Josh elbows me and gives me a stern look. "Dude, I asked you to walk her to her car. What are you still doing with her? I swear if you hurt her, Violet will have my balls in a vise. I told her you were a good guy."

Brody puts his hands up. "Wait a minute. What happened? I missed it."

Josh goes to fill him in, and all I can think is man, we're like a bunch of ol' gossiping men sitting outside the barber shop.

Brody barks a laugh when Josh finishes the story.

"What?" I ask, thinking I missed something.

"Are you kidding right now? Neither one of you know?"

Josh and I look at each other and then at Brody. "Know what?" we both ask.

Brody shakes his head. "You mean to tell me that neither one of you figured it out? Josh, she's your wife, man."

Josh looks perplexed. "What are you talking about?"

"Violet is known for matchmaking. Callie talks about it all the time how she always sets people up and they end up getting married and having babies and all that shit. Violet did that last night on purpose." He points at me. "She was setting you up with April."

Josh's mouth drops, and then he starts to laugh. "I can't believe I didn't figure that out."

I hold my hands up. "Wait. What are you talking about?"

Brody claps me on the shoulder. "You were set up, dude. You better get while the getting's good, or you're going to be married this time next year. I guarantee."

I wait for the shock, fear, or panic to set off, but it doesn't. There's a calm that settles over me. I look over to where I left April, and she's gone. I see Violet over in the corner talking to Callie, but April's nowhere to be seen. "I'll be back," I tell the guys before making the rounds through the big expansive living and dining area. I even go out the back door and search the yard, but she's nowhere to be found. As I come back in, I know I looked panicked. Violet waves at me and points to a door to the side. I go in it, and there sitting at a stool at the kitchen island is April, and there's a boy of around ten sitting next to her, eating a cupcake.

I shake my head. "I swear I can't leave you alone for a minute." It seems no matter the age, boys and men are going to flock to April.

Chapter 9

April

Matt winks at me, and I shrug, smiling. "What can I say? He loves cupcakes, and I was able to sneak him one."

"You're Matt Adams," the boy says, licking the icing from his lips.

Matt ruffles his hair. "Yep. And you must be Trick's son, Calvin."

He nods, eyes wide like he can't believe Matt knows who he is. "You're the best center we've had in a long time."

Matt and I both laugh at that. "Well, thank you..." Matt says.

"Did you see my mom? Was she looking for me? I wasn't supposed to eat sweets before my meal."

Matt shrugs. "I didn't see her."

Calvin gets up from his stool and walks slowly backward toward a door on the other side of the kitchen. "You guys didn't see me." As soon as Matt and I both nod in agreement, he yells. "Thank you for the cupcake, April. See you next season, Matt."

I wave at him, and as soon as he's gone, Matt takes the stool right next to me. "So why you hiding out in here?"

I don't look at him. I can't. I feel like I've already gawked at him across the room, and Violet, Callie, and the other moms all noticed. I'm looking at my fingers, the serving platters set out on the island—heck, I'm looking everywhere but at Matt. "I'm not hiding out. I was letting you do your thing."

He cups my chin in his hand and raises it up so I'm looking at him. "I want you with me."

I shake my head and try to pull away. "No, really, it's fine. Go do your thing. I can entertain myself."

"I want you with me. I asked you to come with me because I knew if you did, I'd have the prettiest woman here on my arm. You can't begrudge me that."

I roll my eyes at him. "Whatever."

He stands up, put his hands on my knees, and slides them up until they're resting on my thighs. My body instantly gravitates to him, and I lean forward. "I'm not joking, April. I want to be with you."

I'm hesitant but finally get up. A part of me is scared, but the other part of me knows that I've promised myself I'd never let a man make me small again. "Fine, I'll go, but you have to promise me one thing."

His answer is immediate. He puts an arm around my shoulder and tucks me against him. "Anything."

I smirk at him, wondering if after what I have to say he's going to make some excuse of why we should leave or something else. "You can't get mad when your friends like me better than you. I'm sort of known as being the life of the party. I'm going to go out there and be me. I'm not holding back."

I'm not trying to scare him off. I'm being honest. Sometimes—well, according to my ex—I can be a lot. I just want to be me, but I still feel like I should warn him. "I wouldn't want you to. I like you... just the way you are."

He definitely knows the right things to say. I walk with him into the other room. *You can do this, April.* I give myself a mental pep talk, and it must work because time flies. We've walked around the room, talking to people. He's introduced me to so many people there's no way I'll remember all their names. But probably the best part is being there with Matt. He never once acts as if I'm not good enough. If anything, he hangs on every word I say. He asks me questions, drawing me into the conversations. And the whole time, he has his hands on me. At first, I'm embarrassed. I've never been big on public displays of affection, but with Matt, it just feels good, and damn, I want to feel good.

We're standing at the back of the room, watching the party happen. It's a typical chaotic three-year-old's birthday party. There are way more adults than kids, but Little B doesn't seem to care. He's loving being the center of attention. Matt is rubbing my back, and his hand slides lower and lower until he's rubbing his palm over my ass.

I bite my lip to hold in the whimper. He leans in, and I inhale his masculine scent. Damn, he even smells fine. I know he used my fruity bodywash, but all I smell is sexy man. His breath hits my cheek. "You about ready to get out of here?"

I can't look at him because if I do, he's going to know exactly what I'm thinking. It's what I've been thinking all day. Him inside me. So instead, I nod, eyes forward.

He presses his lips to my neck, and this time

there's no holding it in. I moan softly and then try to cover it up with a cough.

Matt laughs, enjoying that he knows what he does to me.

We're about to go when Brody waves him over. He looks at me. "Wanna come?"

I cross my arms over my chest so he doesn't see the way my nipples perk up at just his dirty talk. That kiss on the neck surely didn't help matters either.

I know he means more than just going with him to talk to Brody, but I act like I don't have a clue. "No, you go ahead. I'll be right here. I need to say bye to Violet anyway."

He nods, and it's obvious he doesn't want to leave me. "Are you sure? We could go together."

I take a deep breath. He's going out of his way to make me feel welcome and needed, but I don't want him to think I have to tag along when he's talking to his friends. "I'm sure." I laugh when he doesn't move. "Matt, I'm fine. Go ahead. I'll meet you at the front doors."

"Don't go outside without me," he warns.

"Really? I think this neighborhood is safe," I tell him. I mean, I didn't want to gawk, but obviously the

Andrews live in a high-end gated community. I don't think it could get much safer than that.

"Are you kidding? Literally can't leave you alone for a minute. Men of all ages seem to want to be around you. Not that I can blame them."

Oh, this man is good for my ego. "Go, I won't go outside. Brody's waiting."

Finally, he goes. I could have gone, but I need the space. I'm going to spontaneously combust if I spent more time with him nibbling on my ear like he was.

I watch him walk across the room. Damn, I'm getting in over my head.

Chapter 10

Matt

She wasn't kidding. Everyone fell in love with her. She laughed with the other women, and she doesn't seem to know a thing about football, but she entertained the guys by asking questions that were so crazy they were all holding their sides from laughing so hard. And word must have gotten around about her handing out cupcakes, because the kids all sought her out, and she made sure to sneak them each one.

We watched while Little B opened presents and blew out candles, and when everything was about to wind down, we helped Callie clean up.

I walk over to Brody, ready to get out of here. He must see the impatience on my face because he starts in before I get to him. "Forget it."

"Forget what?"

He shakes his head. "Forget my warning. You're already hooked."

I shrug my shoulders, and Brody shrugs. "She's a good one. She fits in, and man, did you see how Little B and all the kids liked her? You better not screw this up."

I shake my head. "I'm not going to screw it up."

But even saying it, I'm worried. Her ex really did a number on her, and he obviously tried to hide the light that is April. How could he not have realized that a woman like that is meant to shine?

I look for April, and Trick is standing next to her. Fuck me. I swear, it's been ten seconds since I left her. From across the room, I can tell she's uncomfortable and trying to cover it up by talking to Calvin. At least I hope she's not interested in Trick. There's a reason he's named that, and it's not because of his plays on the field. "I gotta go, Brody."

I walk over to April, putting my hand on her shoulder and brushing her long black hair away from her face, tucking it behind her ear. "You about ready?"

"Yeah, sure. It was nice to meet you, Trick. I'll see you around, Calvin," she tells them, and I give Trick the look, letting him know she's mine. I've made a point to touch April on the shoulder, or back, or waist. I wanted to reassure her that I wanted her with me, but I also wanted to warn off any of my teammates that were here. If they don't know it by now, they're just idiots, because April's mine. At least I want her to be mine.

We go toward the door. I grab the cake stands from the now empty dessert table. Her cake and cupcakes were a huge hit. We stop long enough to tell Violet and Callie bye, I wave at Josh, and then we're heading out.

I help her into my truck before running around to the driver's side. "Everyone loved the cake and cupcakes."

She answers me softly. "Yeah, they seemed to, didn't they?"

I chuckle. "They did for sure. I'm pretty sure Little B has you wrapped around his finger."

She sighs and looks out the window. "He's a cute kid."

She's quiet, and instead of a comfortable silence, it becomes awkward. For me at least because my mind starts to come up with all kinds of reasons. She leans her head back against the seat and closes her eyes.

I try not to freak out. I've never experienced

anything like this before. I put my arm on the console just to be closer to her. Fuck, I said Little B has her wrapped around his finger. April totally has me wrapped around hers. I'm thinking all kinds of things that I probably shouldn't be.

When I pull into Whiskey Run, April opens her eyes and lifts her head. I sneak a look at her and see her frowning. I break the silence. "What did I do?" I ask her.

She shakes her head but doesn't look at me. "Nothing."

I think back to everything, and then it hits me. "Look, if you're interested in Trick..."

She gives me a look of pure disgust. "I'm not."

I clench the steering wheel. "Did he do something? Say something?"

She crosses her arms over her chest. "Forget it, Matt. It's not a big deal."

I look over at her and have to jerk back onto the road. "What the fuck did he say?"

"Nothing. I'm not even worried about it. I'm used to men like him, Matt. I can handle it."

I lean up in my seat. "Obviously he upset you. You haven't said a word the whole way. Why are you mad if it's not Trick?"

"I'm not mad."

I blow out a breath. "April, talk to me. There's obviously something wrong. I'm about to turn around and go find Trick."

"It's not him."

"Then what is it?"

She takes a deep breath, and I'm waiting for her to fall back into silence, but she surprises me when she starts to ramble. "Look, this is a one-night stand. One night and we're already into night two. You're leaving in a week—well, less than a week; it's four days. I had a good time, but it's over. It is what it is. Right? I mean, this is it. I'm just melancholy, I guess. It's no big deal. Thank you for tonight. I promise that I'll watch more football next season."

Luckily, I'm pulling into her driveway because everything in me tells me to slam on the brakes. As soon as I stop, she grabs her purse and is out the door. "Thank you again for tonight. I had a great time with you."

She is briskly walking away from me, but there's no way I'm letting her go. Fuck!

I get out and slam the truck door and jog after her. I get to her just as she gets the front door unlocked and is about to walk inside. "Matt... please don't make this harder than it is. It was fun. Let's just..."

I put my hand on her shoulder and turn her around to face me. She's staring at my chest, and her eyes are filled with tears. I swear, one little blink and they're overflowing. I know she'll freak out if I tell her what I'm thinking. So I try to keep it casual.

"Four days, April. I don't leave for four days."

She shrugs, and all at once, two big tear drops trail down her cheeks. I cup her face and use my thumbs to wipe them away. "Let's enjoy the next four days."

She starts to argue like I knew she would. "Seriously, if you're asking me to walk away right now, I will, if that's what you really want. But I need you to know that I don't want to. I want to stay."

She sniffles. She's searching my face. "What do you want to do tonight then?"

I push her hair off her face and start to walk her into her house. She's walking backwards, but there's no way I'd let her fall. "I was hoping to get another taste of that pussy... Unless you're too tired."

"No!" she says, and her face turns red. "I mean, I'm not too tired."

I kick the door closed with my boot and walk with her hand in hand to her room.

Chapter 11

April

"She's smiling again," Tara says.

It's one of those random days where Emery, Becca, Tara, and I are all in the bakery together. "I'm a happy person, Becca," I say with a roll of my eyes and then burst into laughter. Quite honestly, I'm not the happy-go-lucky person I'm claiming to be. But it seems the last few days I am. No matter how hard I try, I can't stop smiling.

Emery chimes in. "Yeah, and we all know why you're happy. It's some football player that brings you to work, eats half his weight in pastries, and then takes you home."

"Emery!" I start.

She holds her hands up, laughing. "What? I'm not complaining. This has been our best week."

We all laugh because it's true. Matt definitely loves the treats.

I look over at Becca, and she's the only one that seems distracted. I hate being this happy, especially right now. Her boyfriend broke up with her. He's a dumbass, but we can't help who we like.

Just like I can't help that I like a football player that leaves tomorrow.

My smile instantly drops. I've tried to put it out of my mind all day long, but I can't. Matt is leaving tomorrow. We've spent every possible minute together when I haven't been at work. Being with him has me hoping for things I shouldn't be hoping for, but try and tell that to my heart.

I rub my palm over my chest, right over my heart. Darn, tomorrow's going to suck.

Tara points out the door. "Speaking of the football players. Get ready. Incoming."

All eyes go toward the big windows. Matt, Josh, and a few of the other guys I recognize from the party the other night are about to cross the street, heading this way.

Emery heads to the back. "I better restock real quick."

She no sooner gets into the kitchen than Matt leads the rest of the guys in.

"Hey," I say as soon as he walks in.

His eyes land on mine as if he was searching for me, and he smiles real big. "Hey yourself, honey."

I start to fan myself and stop when I realize what I'm doing.

Tara laughs and mockingly starts to fan herself. Becca is busy at the island, decorating some cookies, so I step forward. "How'd it go at the diner?"

"We got everything moved that Violet wanted moved. She even fed us. But don't worry, we all saved enough room for a cupcake... or two."

The guys all crowd around the display case and put in their orders. Every day I've tried to give Matt free pastries, but he won't let me. He insists on paying, telling me they're worth it.

I hand him the little box with two cupcakes in it. He takes them and juts his chin out at me. "Now give me what I really want."

I roll my eyes and lean in to kiss him on the cheek, but he's way too fast for me. He turns his head, and my lips meet his. Our kiss, like every other time, goes from sweet and innocent to frenzied and frantic in a second. I break away, and all eyes are on us, but Matt doesn't notice. "Now that's what I'm talking about," he says with a low whistle.

My whole body heats not just because everyone is watching us but because this is just how my body reacts to him. I've never had anyone make me feel the way he does. Yes, I'm plus size, and it took me many years to learn to love my body. It was instant for him. He insists on showing me every night just how much he likes it.

The guys are all thanking us and heading toward the door. "I gotta go. But I'll be back in an hour to pick you up."

I nod. "Tomorrow..." I start and stop. I don't even know what I was going to say. I can't tell him to stay. We've known each other for less than a week. It would be ridiculous... even though it's what I want to do.

He puts his hands on my shoulders and grips me tightly. "Look at me."

I lift my head, trying to hide the pain I'm feeling. I don't want him to feel guilty. We both knew what this was.

He doesn't look sad, and it sort of irks me. Shouldn't he be upset that he's leaving? He cups my cheek, searching my face with a soft smile on his lips. "We'll talk about it tonight, okay?"

I nod, and he kisses me one more time before heading out with the guys.

Tara, like a parrot, comes to stand next to me. "She's not smiling now, guys."

Emery and Becca come over. These women are my best friends. We'd do anything for each other, and I know when I fall apart, they're going to be there to help pick up the pieces. I suck in a breath. It's just that this time is different. I know the pain is going to be like nothing I've ever felt before.

Becca, who has her own heartache, doesn't offer me any reassurance. She just loops her arm in mine. "I'll be there for you no matter what. Just like you've done for me." I nod. I've hated watching Becca hurt like she has. There's never been any doubt that she deserved better than her ex. He never treated her right. I hold on to her a little tighter. I've been in her shoes and let a man treat me wrong, and I can preach to her until I'm blue in the face, but she's going to have to realize it and make it happen on her own.

Tara, the youngest of all of us, seems to still believe in fairy tales. "There's no way that man is leaving. He's totally gaga for you, April."

I turn and look at her with hope in my eyes. I wish I could believe what she's saying, but I'm not going to get my hopes up.

Emery comes to stand on the other side of me

and hits her hip to mine. "You need to talk to him... ask him to stay."

She's been there, done that, and got the trophy for it. She's been married... to the man of her dreams the way she talks about him. But they're divorced now. It's obvious to everyone that Emery's looking for someone exactly like Nash, her ex. I would never admit it to her, but I'm still holding out hope that she and Nash can work it out. It's obvious the man still loves her by the way he's always lurking around here. I shake my head. "I can't ask him to stay. His family is in Texas."

Emery shakes her head. "They'll still be his family if he lives here."

I put my hand on my hip and point out the window where we can see Matt and the other guys walking down the sidewalk. "We met just a few days ago."

Emery grabs me by the shoulders. "That doesn't matter."

I'm ready to argue with her, but she shakes her head. "Think about how he makes you feel. Then tell me if you're ready to not feel that anymore. And be honest with yourself. You don't have to tell me or Tara or Becca, but be honest with yourself. Do you want to lose him and not even let him know what you're feeling or what you're thinking?"

Her words hit home. I know she's right. I can just tell him. Maybe we can still talk or we can visit each other. It doesn't have to be completely over. He'll be here next season if nothing else. "Okay, I'll talk to him."

The girls are all happy. Tara instantly starts shaking her hips, dancing across the checkerboard floor. Becca is happy for me. She hugs me and then gets back to work. It's almost time for Emery and me to leave for the day, and so for the next hour, I try to figure out what I need to say to him.

If he goes or stays, I'm going to at least make sure he knows what I'm feeling. I owe myself that.

Chapter 12

Matt

I know I'm making the right decision. I put the plans into motion the third day after I met April. Some would say I'm crazy, but I don't care. I have to follow my heart on this one. The only thing that's freaking me out is what is April going to say? But I've made this decision, and even if she's not happy with it, I'm not giving up.

She's leaning against the brick wall of the bakery when I pull up. I jump out and run around to open the door for her. "Sorry I'm late."

She walks toward me, smiling. "It's okay. I should have driven. I'm sure you have a lot to do tonight."

I kiss her and help her into the truck, ignoring

her comment. There is a lot I still need to do, but it can wait.

I grunt instead of agreeing with her. Now that it's here, I'm nervous. I go back to my side and climb in. "What do you want for dinner?"

She shakes her head. "I don't care. I'm not really that hungry."

I shift in my seat as I pull out of the parking lot. "I ate at Red's and then had those cupcakes. But you need to eat something."

She shrugs. "It's fine. I can fix a sandwich at home."

I drive us to her house, our hands on the console between us. Our fingers are threaded together. It takes mere minutes, but it seems longer since we're both so quiet. She clears her throat as we pull in. "Uh, there's something I wanted to talk to you about."

I squeeze her hand. "Me too. I mean, there's something I wanted to talk to you about."

"You first," she says.

I take a deep breath. "Can we go in? Maybe sit on the couch and talk for a minute?"

She nods and lets go of my hand. I follow behind her with my hands shaking. I can do this. I have to do this.

We get inside, and she puts her purse down and goes to the couch. Her back is ramrod straight, and for the first time, I realize she's on edge too. "You're nervous."

She lets out a breath and giggles softly. "Well, yeah, I guess I am."

I take a deep breath and sit down next to her. I sit close so our legs are touching. I wrap my hands around both hers. She leans toward me, and I'm staring at her. Dare I say, she's looking at me with hopefulness on her face. Fuck, I hope I'm right.

"I don't know how to say it, so I'm just going to say it."

She leans back a little, and I hold her hands tighter. "I'm not leaving."

Her mouth falls open. "You're not leaving? What does that mean, you're not leaving? Like now, tomorrow? Are you leaving next week?"

Her questions are quickfire, but she's still frowning at me. I scoot closer and clear my throat, searching her eyes, hoping to see some hint that she's happy about this. "No, I'm not leaving at all. I'm moving to Whiskey Run. Josh found me an apartment in town. I'm signing the lease tomorrow, and then I'll move out of my apartment in Jasper. I mean, I'll be here until spring training starts. I'll have to travel with the team for games and all that, but I'm making Whiskey Run my home base."

She opens her mouth and then closes it. Then does the same thing again. I'm on the edge of my seat, grasping for something. "Say it. What are you thinking?"

She blinks. "Well, you must really like Whiskey Run to move here."

I shake my head. She still doesn't get it. "No. I mean I like Whiskey Run, but the correct way to say it is I must really love you to move here."

She gasps. "You love me? But we just met..."

I shrug. That same thing has crossed my mind. "I told myself the same thing, but you know what? It doesn't matter. I know how I feel, April, and I love you. I can't leave you and go to Texas. Fuck, I hate being away from you during the day. I can't imagine not seeing you."

She's speechless, and I try to keep myself calm. "I know it's fast, and I know you may not be ready. There's no pressure. I just want you to give us a chance."

She moves quickly into my lap, and I hold on to her as she blurts out, "Move in here."

Her arms are around my neck, and I have to lean back to see her face. "Move in here?"

She nods quickly. "You haven't signed the lease yet... I mean you don't have to... I just thought—"

I grip my hands on to her waist. "I didn't want to pressure you... I want you to be sure."

She takes a deep breath. "I'm sure. That's the thing I was going to tell you... the thing I wanted to talk to you about."

"You were going to invite me to move in?"

She shakes her head. "No, I really didn't get that far. I was going to tell you how I felt. I didn't think I had the right to make you choose between me and being with your family."

I nod even though I don't agree with her logic. She has the right to everything as far as I'm concerned. "Okay, so tell me."

Her eyes widen, and she starts to stutter. "I uh, I planned it all out but uh..."

I don't want to make her nervous. "It's okay, you don't have—"

But she interrupts me. "I love you. I was going to tell you that, and then I was going to suggest we still see each other. I checked on times I could come to Texas, and I thought you could come visit too."

I push the hair away from her face and hold the side of her head. "I like that first part. I love hearing you say the words. But not the second part. It's not an option for me, April. I can't be that far away from you."

"So move in."

"Are you sure?"

She doesn't even hesitate. "Yes, I'm sure. I love you, Matt. I want us to be together." She bites her lower lip. "But your family is going to hate me for taking you from them."

I pull her to me and lie back on the couch, cradling her head on my chest. "They're not going to hate you. They're going to love you. They just want me happy, and you make me happy."

She rests her chin on my chest and looks up at me. "You make me happy too."

"Plus... eventually, when you're ready for it, I want you to be my family too."

Her eyes darken. "Yeah, I like that."

I rub my hands up and down her back. "So we should probably celebrate, don't you think?"

"Oh yeah? What are you thinking?" she asks.

Before she can even get it all out, I'm cupping her between the thighs. "You know what I want."

Her hips jerk. "Me too."

I pull her up the length of my body, and we're molded together. None of the decisions I've made were made lightly. I truly believe that April's the one. "I love you."

She nods. "I know." She pushes off me and stands up, holding her hand out. "Come on, big boy, I'm going to let you prove it to me."

I jump up and chase her to the bedroom. I'm going to prove it to her. Over and over, until she feels so loved, so cherished there's absolutely no doubt in her mind we belong together. I don't care if it takes forever.

Epilogue

April

I can barely contain myself. It's been a month since Matt made the decision to stay in Whiskey Run. He spends his days working out with the guys from his team that live in Jasper and doing marketing spots and interviews.

He had to travel out of town last weekend, and it was pure hell. He definitely made the right decision in staying here. We would have been miserable apart.

Tonight I told him I had a surprise for him, and we traveled the hour to Whiskey Valley. We have our friends with us. Violet and Josh are here. Emery and Becca came, and it thrilled me that we were finally able to get Becca out of the house. Too bad

Tara couldn't make it, but she had plans with her boyfriend.

Right now, were standing in the stands at the big indoor arena. We stopped beforehand and had dinner at the Sunrise Diner and then came straight here. I cheer loudly for the guy that just made eight seconds. I don't know a lot about this, but I know that's what they're trying to do. When I sit back down, I notice that Matt is sitting quietly beside me, and I nudge his shoulder. "You don't like your surprise?"

He sits up straighter. "This is my surprise?"

I try to hide the hurt from my face. "You don't like it?"

He grabs my hand. "Talk to me. Why'd you think I would like this?"

"Well, it's a sport. You like sports. You're from Texas, and I figured you were missing this type of thing, so I planned for you and all our friends to come... You don't like it."

He leans down and kisses me. It's hot, and I rest my hand on his chest until he pulls away and his voice is thick. "I like it now."

My forehead creases, not understanding. "You didn't, though?"

"Honey, I'll be honest with you. Don't think I'm

psycho or trying to control you or whatever, but I don't like my woman cheering for other men." He shrugs his shoulder. "Now that you explained it, I appreciate what you've done, but I have to tell you, even when I lived in Texas, I never went to these things. I was always on the football field."

"I'm sorry, I wasn't even thinking..."

He leans down and presses his forehead to mine. "Honestly, I was really thinking you had a different surprise for me."

I laugh and look around at our friends who are trying to act like they're not being completely nosy and listening to everything we say. Good thing it's loud in here. My hands go to Matt's waist. "Oh yeah? What did you want the surprise to be?"

He turns my head and presses his lips to my ear. His hot breath is like a soft tickle. "That you were going to tell me you were pregnant."

I gasp and look up him. "No way!" I slap him on the chest and then my eyes get even bigger. "Oh my God, you're not joking!"

He shakes his head, and by the look on his face, I know he's being serious right now. "But... but..." I pull him away from the others and grab his shirt to get him closer to me. "We always use something... It's so soon... Are you serious right now?"

He laughs. "I'm definitely serious about you. And yes, I want to get married and have babies with you. Preferably in that order."

His words send a tremble down my spine. I'm already imaging Matt as a father, and I know he'd be a great one. "Well, I guess it's a good thing I'm not pregnant then since we're not..." I stop and put my hands to my mouth when Matt steps out into the aisle and gets down on one knee.

A hush falls around us. "April, I love you, and I want to spend the rest of my life with you. I don't care where I'm at, what I'm doing, I want you by my side. Will you please do me the honor of being my wife? Marry me, honey, so I can put some babies in you."

I laugh because how could I not? But I also drop to my knees in front of him. "Yes! Yes! Yes!"

He puts the ring on my finger, cups my face, and presses his lips to mine. The kiss is everything, telling me how much he loves me and that even though we haven't been together long, I know he's my soul mate.

When we finally pull apart, everyone is whooping and hollering. They have us up on the Jumbotron, and our friends are all clapping and cheering.

I'm smiling ear to ear as the girls all gather

around me. "You knew, didn't you?" I say to Violet, Becca, and Emery, and they're all nodding their heads.

Each one of them hug and congratulate me as the guys all slap Matt on the back. He's not away from me long, though. He comes back over to stand next to me, and I can't help looking at him in awe. He's really mine. I put my hand over my chest. I've never been so happy.

"I was trying to surprise you, and you surprised me instead."

He laughs as his hand runs up and down my back. "I thought for sure one of your friends would tell you."

I hold my hand out and look at the diamond on my finger. "I didn't have a clue." I look up at him. "So you ready to get out of here?"

"No way, honey. Now that you have my ring on your finger, I feel way better. You can cheer on whoever as long as you're by my side."

I sit cuddled under his arm as we watch the next ride. Becca excuses herself and climbs down the bleachers. I look at Emery, and she explains by mouthing *bathroom* to me.

I nod and settle back in. Two rides go by, and Becca's still not back. "I hope Becca's okay."

As soon as the words leave my mouth, Becca's walking back toward us with a cowboy hot on her tail. Her face is red, and I can't help but watch curiously. The cowboy is obviously one of the riders. He's covered in dirt and in full gear, chaps and all, but that doesn't stop him from climbing up the bleachers behind Becca. He stops and wait for her to sit down between Violet and Emery.

He takes his hat off and holds it to his chest. "You okay now?"

Becca juts her chin out. "Yeah, I'm fine. Just embarrassed. You didn't have to carry me."

Emery gasps. "Becca! Are you okay? What happened?"

Becca shakes her head. "I tripped coming from the bathroom, and then there was a stampede of people that tried to get by me. This guy"—she points at the cowboy—"decided the best course of action was to pick me up and try to carry me back to my seat."

The blond cowboy smiles. "It was my pleasure, Becca." He seems pleased, drawing out her name. He must have tried to get it, and Becca wasn't giving it.

She looks at Emery and presses her lips together

and then her teeth when she looks at the cowboy again. "I wasn't thanking you."

The dirty look doesn't even faze him. "It was still my pleasure."

The announcers come over the speaker. "Up next is a fan favorite. We're going to take a little break, and then Lucas Granger will be riding Rampage. Hold on to your hats, it's going to be a helluva ride."

"That's you!" Emery says, pointing up at the Jumbotron.

The cowboy turns and then looks back with a smile. "Yep, it is." He points at Becca. "You going to wish me luck?"

Becca rolls her eyes, clearly not falling for the cowboy. "Sure, good luck," she drawls.

He just laughs. He puts one foot on the higher step and leans over. "So how about a wager?"

We're all looking between Lucas and Becca. He's completely, one hundred percent, enamored with her, and she looks as if she's bored. Even though her cheeks do have a slight tinge to them.

"I'm not making a bet with you."

He shakes his head. "Not a bet. But how about if I stay on Rampage the eight seconds, you'll give me your number?"

Becca looks surprised but recovers quickly. "Sorry, but I'm not interested."

He stands up to his full height. "Well, at least stick around and watch. I have a feeling you're going to be my good luck charm."

She shrugs, and Lucas puts his hat back on his head. "I'll see you later, Becca. It was nice seein' you all. Thanks for coming out."

He walks down the steps, and all eyes are on Becca until she starts to squirm. "What? You all about ready to go?"

I laugh. "You can't leave yet. You may just be his good luck charm."

She ignores me, and it doesn't take long for Lucas to get down to the arena and up in the starting point. The bull he's riding is huge and already mad. The countdown is quick, and before we know it, the shute opens, and Lucas and the bull come barreling out. He holds on, and while everyone's watching him, I'm watching Becca. She's interested. It's plainly written on her face as she scoots forward, watching from the edge of her seat. When the eight seconds are over, we all jump up, even Becca, and cheer. It was phenomenal.

And Lucas stands up on the rings of the fence and points up to Becca and then holds his fingers to his ear like he's holding a phone. He wants her number.

"Okay, that's enough. Eyes on me," Matt says, kissing the side of my neck.

I turn. "Take me home."

He squints. "If you want to stay..."

I shake my head. "Nope, I have no doubt in my mind that Violet's going to make sure that cowboy gets Becca's number. It's time for us to go." I wiggle my eyebrows at him.

He normally laughs at my antics, but not this time. He grabs my hand. "We're leaving, guys."

He all but drags me down the steps as we holler bye at everyone. "In a hurry?" I ask him.

"In a hurry to make our engagement official."

I loop my arm through his as he navigates us through the crowd of people. "And how do you plan to do that?"

As soon as we get out the door and are on the way to the truck, I ask him again. "Huh, what's your plan? How are you making this official?"

He stops next to his truck, opens the door, and helps me inside. He leans across me, pulling the seatbelt over me and locking it into place. He stares straight into my eyes. "I hope you plan on a short engagement because I'm making it official by putting a baby into you tonight."

Breathless, all I can do is nod my head. "I like the way you think." I cup his cheek. "I'm not going to make it the hour to the house."

He smiles. "That's why I got a hotel room for tonight. We'll be there in five minutes."

"You spoil me, Matt."

He kisses me. "And I plan to for the rest of our lives."

He jogs around to the other side of the truck and gets in beside me. He gets pulled out on the road and threads our fingers together on the console between us, and I finally put voice to my thoughts. "How did I get so lucky?"

He chuckles. "I'm the lucky one."

———

Want Lucas and Becca's story?
Read it in Rebound Love.
mybook.to/ReboundLoveHopeFord

Whiskey Run Series

Want more of Whiskey Run?

Whiskey Run

Faithful - He's the hot, say-it-like-it-is cowboy, and he won't stop until he gets the woman he wants.

Captivated - She's a beautiful woman on the run... and I'm going to be the one to keep her.

Obsessed - She's loved him since high school and now he's back.

Seduced - He's a football player that falls in love with the small town girl.

Devoted - She's a plus size model and he's a small town mechanic.

Whiskey Run: Savage Ink

Virile - He won't let her go until he puts his mark on her.

Torrid - He'll do anything to give her what she wants.

Rigid - If you love reading about emotionally wounded men and the women that help them overcome their past, then you'll love Dawson and Emily's story.

Whiskey Run: Cowboys Love Curves

Obsessed Cowboy - She's the preacher's daughter and she's

off limits.

Whiskey Run: Heroes

Ransom - He's on a mission he can't lose.

Redeem - He's in love with his sister's best friend.

Submit - She's his fake wife but he wants to make it real.

Forbid - They have a secret romance but he's about to stake his claim.

Whiskey Run: Sugar

One Night Love - Her one night stand wants more.

Rebound Love - She's falling for the rebound guy.

Second Chance Love - He is not a man to ignore... especially when he asks for a second chance.

Bad Boy Love - He's a bad boy that wants her good.

Free Books

Want FREE BOOKS?

Go to www.authorhopeford.com/freebies

JOIN ME!

JOIN MY NEWSLETTER & READERS GROUP

www.AuthorHopeFord.com/Subscribe

JOIN MY READERS GROUP ON FACEBOOK

www.FB.com/groups/hopeford

Find Hope Ford at www.authorhopeford.com

About the Author

USA Today Bestselling Author Hope Ford writes short, steamy, sweet romances. She loves tattooed, alpha men, instant love stories, and ALWAYS happily ever afters. She has over 100 books and they are all available on Amazon.

To find me on Pinterest, Instagram, Facebook, Goodreads, and more:

www.AuthorHopeFord.com/follow-me

Printed in Great Britain
by Amazon